Leopards

Leopards

Karen Povey

KIDHAVEN PRESS

An imprint of Thomson Gale, a part of The Thomson Corporation

THOMSON
™
GALE

Detroit • New York • San Francisco • San Diego • New Haven, Conn.
Waterville, Maine • London • Munich

© 2005 Thomson Gale, a part of The Thomson Corporation.

Thomson and Star Logo are trademarks and Gale and KidHaven Press are registered trademarks used herein under license.

For more information, contact
KidHaven Press
27500 Drake Rd.
Farmington Hills, MI 48331-3535
Or you can visit our Internet site at http://www.gale.com

LIBRARY OF CONGRESS CATALOGING-IN-PUBLICATION DATA

Povey, Karen D., 1962-
  Leopards / by Karen Povey.
    p. cm. — (Nature's predators)
  ISBN 0-7377-2348-3 (hardback : alk. paper)
  I. Title. II. Series.
  QL737.C23P692 2004
  599.75'54—dc22

                              2004007488

Printed in the United States of America

CONTENTS

CHAPTER ONE

Powerful Predators

S ome of the most well-known predators in nature are the wild cats. Cats are perfectly built for catching, killing, and eating other animals. Among the most fierce and skillful hunters in the wild cat family are the leopards. Because of their amazing strength and secretive ways, leopards are often thought of as the best predators of all.

There are three wild cats that have the word "leopard" as part of their name: the leopard, the clouded leopard, and the snow leopard. All of these leopards are different kinds of animal, or **species**, in the cat family. They are powerfully built cats with fairly short legs, spotted coats, and long, thick tails. Although they are alike in many ways, they also have some important differences.

The Leopard

The leopard, sometimes called the common leopard, can be found in many different places. Leopards live in Africa, Asia, and the Middle East. They make their homes in forests, grasslands, and even deserts. Not all leopards look alike. Depending on where they live, leopards have slightly different coat colors ranging from pale yellow to dark gold. A leopard's coat color helps it to blend in with the background so it can easily hide while it hunts. Leopards living in deserts and grasslands have lighter-colored coats to match the sand and dried grass. Those living in forests have darker coats that help them blend into the dark plants and shadows.

The pattern of spots on a common leopard's coat is called a rosette.

The coats of most leopards are covered by a special pattern of black spots arranged in a circle. This pattern is called a **rosette**. Some leopards are born with all-black coats. These black leopards, known as **panthers**, still have rosettes, but they are faint and difficult to see. Black leopards are usually found living in forests where their dark color helps them to hide.

Besides having coats of different colors, leopards can also be different sizes. Small female leopards may weigh only fifty-five pounds, while large males may be nearly two hundred pounds. Leopards living in tropical forests are usually the smallest. Their smaller size helps them move more easily through the trees. The largest leopards, called Amur leopards, live in Russia. Their large size is important because it helps them stay warm in the cold Russian winter.

The Clouded Leopard

Much smaller than the Amur leopard, the clouded leopard lives in the tropic Southeast Asia. The clouded leopard weighs only twenty-five to forty-five pounds. Its small size allows the clouded leopard to be very quick and agile as it moves through the trees. The clouded leopard is an amazing tree climber. Its short legs provide great strength for running up branches. Using its three-foot-long tail for balance, this acrobatic cat can climb headfirst down a tree or hang underneath the branches.

Instead of rosettes, clouded leopards have larger, blotchy spots shaped like clouds. The shape of these

The clouded leopard is much smaller than other types of leopards.

spots give the clouded leopard its name. Clouded leopards are extremely shy and secretive cats. Because they are so difficult to observe in the wild, very little is known about their habits. Scientists are still trying to learn basic information about this species, such as how it hunts and what it eats.

The Snow Leopard

The snow leopard is another champion climber. However, unlike the clouded leopard or common leopard, the snow leopard is never found in the trees. Instead, this high-climbing cat scales the cliffs and crags of its home in the mountains of central Asia. The snow leopard is specially designed to live in such a harsh and cold environment. Its thick grayish-white coat keeps it warm in freezing temperatures and blowing snow.

Its large paws act as snowshoes, helping the snow leopard walk across drifts of snow. These large feet also provide a good grip for the cat as it moves over loose rock on high mountain meadows. While resting, the snow leopard wraps its long, fluffy tail around its face like a scarf to warm the air that it breathes.

The snow leopard's tail also helps it balance as it leaps along rock ledges. Snow leopards can make leaps up to thirty feet across. This ability makes them the best jumpers in the cat family.

Built for Meat Eating

Despite differences in how they look and the places they live, all three species of leopards have a great deal in common. All leopards are **carnivores**, or meat-eating animals. Leopards are powerful cats that hunt

The snow leopard has large paws, which make it easier to run across snow.

Leopard Anatomy

Keen eyesight and the ability to see in the dark enable the leopard to hunt at night.

Spotted fur helps the leopard hide as it sneaks up on its prey.

Razor-sharp claws are sheathed within the paws until they are needed.

Strong legs enable the leopard to run as fast as thirty miles per hour over short distances.

prey, animals that may be two or even three times larger than they are. To successfully catch and kill such large animals, leopards have tremendous strength. Leopards are very muscular cats that are able to hold onto large, strong animals and wrestle them to the ground.

Leopards also have very powerful jaws that allow them to kill and eat their prey. In those strong jaws are thirty teeth. Leopards have three main types of teeth. A leopard's long, sharp **canine teeth**, or fangs, help it grab and kill prey. The clouded leopards has especially long canine teeth. In fact, for its size, the clouded leopard has the longest canine teeth of any cat. For this reason, the clouded leopard is sometimes known as the modern-day saber-toothed cat.

To eat its prey, a leopard uses special molars along the sides of its jaws. These molars are called **carnassial teeth**. Carnassial teeth have extremely sharp edges and work like the blades of scissors to cut through meat as the leopard bites down. When a leopard eats, it doesn't actually chew the meat. The leopard swallows pieces of meat whole instead.

The third type of teeth in a leopard's mouth are the **incisors**. Incisors are the teeth at the very front of the jaws. These teeth are very small and play only a slight role in hunting. They provide more gripping power for a leopard's jaws and may also be used to nibble small bits of meat from bones.

All together, the leopards' great strength, powerful jaws, and special teeth allow these amazing cats to be some of nature's most successful predators.

CHAPTER TWO

On the Prowl

Although leopards live in many different places and **habitats**, they all hunt in much the same way. Leopards do not catch their prey by running after animals they see in the distance. Most prey animals are faster than leopards and would easily escape when they saw the cat coming. Instead, leopards hunt by **ambushing** their prey. In ambush hunting, a leopard will slowly sneak up on, or **stalk**, its prey before making a sudden attack.

Finding Prey

A leopard begins its hunt by looking for prey. Leopards usually hunt when their prey is most active. Most prey animals come out at night or around sunrise and sunset to eat, drink, and move about. Therefore leopards are mostly **nocturnal**, searching for their prey during the night. During the day, both leopards and their prey are usually resting.

Leopards have excellent senses to help them find their prey in the dark of night. The main sense leopards use while hunting is their eyesight. Leopards can see well even in the dark. A leopard's large eyes need only a tiny bit of light, such as moonlight, to be able to see. Like most nocturnal animals, leopards do not see in color. Color vision is not possible in the dark. A leopard's eyes are best at spotting movement, so even the slightest motion of grass or leaves may alert a leopard to nearby prey.

Leopards also have very sensitive hearing. They can hear sounds so faint that a human would never notice them. During a hunt, a leopard can listen for

Highly developed senses of sight and hearing make the leopard an effective hunter.

Leopards prefer to hunt their prey at night. Here, a leopard drags an antelope it has killed.

the sounds of prey rustling leaves or walking across a rocky cliff. Leopards are able to move their ears in all directions without moving their heads. This helps a leopard listen for prey without making movements that might frighten the animal away.

Leopards also have a good sense of smell. Leopards do not use this sense much for hunting, but may sometimes sniff a trail to learn if prey has passed by.

Staying Hidden

Once a leopard locates prey, it will begin its stalk. During a stalk a leopard must be very careful to approach its prey quietly and slowly. Prey animals such as deer, wild sheep, and monkeys, are extremely alert and cautious. They will immediately run off if they hear any sounds or see any movement that tells them a leopard is nearby.

Leopards stalk their prey with great care and patience. Holding perfectly still, the cat will move only when it is sure it will not be seen. When a leopard does move toward its prey, it takes slow and quiet footsteps that will not be noticed. Leopards move with such smoothness that their bodies almost seem to melt through their surroundings.

A leopard's coat provides the **camouflage** it needs to stay hidden during its stalk. The color and design of a leopard's coat allow it to blend in to its habitat, causing it to nearly disappear from view. The leopard's spot

A leopard carefully stalks its prey in the tall grasses of the African savanna.

pattern breaks up the outline of its body, making it difficult to tell the difference between the leopard and a shadow.

Because leopards do not live in pairs or groups, they hunt alone. If a mother leopard has young cubs, she will leave them in a hiding spot when she goes to look for food. A successful hunt depends on the leopard taking its prey by surprise. Cubs would likely make noise and alert the prey if they came along on the hunt. Only when the cubs are old enough to learn how to hunt will the mother bring them along.

Leopard Prey

Although leopards hunt in mostly the same way, the types of prey they hunt may be quite different. Leopards are not picky eaters and between them will hunt just about any animal they can find. Of the three leopard species, common leopards have the most variety in their diets. Scientists know that these leopards eat almost any type of animal, from insects and birds to very large hoofed animals such as deer and antelope. Scientists think that

The coloring and pattern of spots on the coat of the common leopard (opposite page) and snow leopard (left) help them blend into their surroundings.

this wide menu is one reason why common leopards can live in so many different places.

Most leopards eat some type of hoofed animal. The snow leopard's favorite prey is a type of wild sheep called the bharal, or blue sheep. The snow leopard also hunts wild goats called ibex and markhor. These animals are very alert and sure-footed, making it difficult for a snow leopard to sneak up on and capture one. To make matters worse, snow leopards must hunt these goats and sheep on very steep cliff faces and meadows where there are few places to hide. Therefore, the snow leopard's camouflage is extremely important for a successful hunt. The snow leopard's smoky-gray coat helps it hide behind boulders and in the shadows of cliffs during its stalk. Often, however, the snow leopard's prey will see it coming and escape.

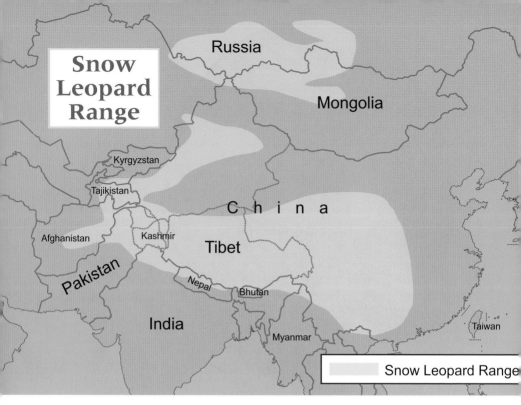

Although it is much smaller than the common leopard and snow leopard, the clouded leopard is also able to hunt large prey such as deer and wild pigs. They are also known to eat smaller animals such as porcupines, squirrels, and other rodents. However, because clouded leopards are such secretive cats, scientists know very little about their hunting habits. No one has ever watched a clouded leopard stalking prey. Scientists think that because clouded leopards are such skilled climbers, they may do some of their hunting in the treetops, catching monkeys, squirrels, and birds.

Using its patience and camouflage, a leopard will find its target and close in for the kill. If it is lucky, it will be successful and enjoy a well-earned meal.

CHAPTER THREE

Killer Instinct

Once a stalking leopard has gotten as close to its prey as possible without being seen, it is time for the attack. If a leopard is able to get very close to its prey, it may be able to make a single pounce, or leap, and catch the animal by surprise. If the prey is not within pouncing distance, however, the leopard must complete its ambush by running toward its prey.

The Attack

The leopard will begin its attack with a fast and sudden leap from its hiding place. In response, its prey will quickly bolt away. The leopard must use all its speed and strength to catch its prey before it escapes. Over a short distance, leopards are fast. Leopards can run about thirty miles per hour, but this speed does not last for long. If the leopard does not catch up to its

A leopard can pounce more than twenty feet to catch its prey.

fleeing prey within a few seconds, it will become too tired and have to give up the chase.

Leopards have very flexible bodies that help them move with a strong burst of speed. A leopard's backbone can bend and stretch to help send its legs zooming over the ground. Freely moving shoulder blades allow leopards to reach their front legs way out to cover long distances as they rush closer to their prey.

As they try to escape, animals such as deer and wild sheep often run in a zigzag pattern to try to avoid the chasing cat. The leopard will throw its long tail from side to side to help it keep up with the sharp turns. The snow leopard will even use its tail as a brake to help it stop when it reaches its prey. By throwing its heavy tail straight into the air, the snow leopard can slow down quickly to keep from tumbling down a steep mountainside.

Making the Kill

As the leopard catches up to its prey it will make one final, powerful leap and grab it. The leopard will extend its razor-sharp claws that, up until that moment, had been hidden within its paws. By staying inside the leopard's paws most of the time, these **retractable claws** remain sharp for grabbing and holding onto prey. If a leopard's claws were always sticking out of

A leopard stretches out its body as it prepares to pounce on prey from a tree branch.

its paws, like those of a dog, they would wear down and become dull and useless as hunting weapons.

The leopard's claws will sink into its prey, holding it steady. If the prey is small, the leopard will quickly kill it by biting it at the back of the neck. The leopard's long canine teeth are perfectly shaped for slipping between the neck bones of an animal, allowing the leopard to make a quick, killing bite that cuts through the spinal cord.

However, if the prey is large, such as a deer or antelope, the kill will be more difficult. It will take all of the leopard's strength to keep a grip as the animal struggles to escape. When capturing large prey, leopards will usually try to bite the animal on the throat. This may be very difficult since the animal may be fighting back wildly with thrashing hooves and stabbing horns. In fact, leopards are often injured by the prey that they hunt. Leopards must be extremely tough to hold onto and overpower such large and dangerous animals.

If the leopard is able to bite its prey on the throat, it will hold on tightly with its long canine teeth in an attempt to cut off the animal's air supply and suffocate it. Unable to breathe, the prey will weaken its struggle quickly. After a few minutes, it will die.

The Feast

If the leopard had to struggle to kill its prey, it will be exhausted afterward. The cat may rest a short while, but will soon turn its attention to eating its kill. Very

A leopard sharpens its claws by scratching a tree. Its claws stay retracted until the leopard kills its prey.

small prey may be devoured whole, in just one or two bites. Birds are usually plucked of their feathers before being eaten.

Larger prey takes longer for a leopard to eat. Sometimes a leopard will drag its kill out of sight underneath some bushes or trees, where it can eat without being disturbed. Leopards usually prefer to begin feeding on the rear part of the body, or carcass, of large animals. This area of the carcass has a great deal of muscle meat, which the leopard prefers. Sometimes a leopard will begin eating at the belly because the animal's hide is easier to bite into there.

Because catching a large animal is so difficult, leopards that are successful will eat a large meal, or **gorge**, after such a kill. A large leopard or snow leopard might eat as much as twenty pounds of meat at one time.

A common leopard kills a gazelle with a powerful bite to the neck that severs the animal's spinal cord.

Clouded leopards, being smaller, would eat much less at one sitting.

The leopard will eat almost the entire kill. Only the stomach, intestines, skull, and large bones remain when the meal is over. The leopard uses its rough tongue to lick every last bit of meat from the bones. If the carcass is too large to eat at one time, the leopard may try to hide it for later by covering the kill with leaves or dirt.

Caching Food

Common leopards, especially those living on the grasslands of Africa, often have to worry about competition from other predators when they feed from their kill. After using so much energy and skill to catch their prey, leopards may be the victims of other carnivores trying to steal their kill. Lions and hyenas, in particular, are attracted to the sights and sounds of a leopard's kill. They will take any opportunity to drive the leopard away so they can claim an easy meal.

Leopards will rarely fight with lions or hyenas to protect their kill. Those animals might injure or kill a leopard. Instead, leopards protect their kill by placing it out of reach. Leopards will often drag the carcass into the branches of a tree to keep it safe. This habit is called **caching** their food. Once the kill is safe, the leopard can eat its meal without being bothered by other animals. Caching requires enormous strength because the leopard must carry a carcass that might be two or three times the leopard's own weight high into the

A leopard in South Africa feeds undisturbed on a carcass it has hidden in the branches of a tree.

trees. For this reason, leopards are often considered to be the world's strongest cat species.

The Next Hunt

When leopards hunt small prey, such as rodents or monkeys, they may have to hunt every day, or even several times each day. However, leopards that are able to catch and kill large prey are able to spend time resting between hunts. Because they are able to eat so much food at one time, they might not need to hunt again for another week or even longer. One scientist determined that a snow leopard kills a large prey animal once every ten to fifteen days.

Not every hunt is successful, however. Leopards use a great deal of time and energy stalking and chasing prey that escapes. Only the most skillful leopards will be able to catch enough food to survive.

CHAPTER FOUR

Leopards in Danger

Because leopards are such powerful predators, they rarely face danger from other animals. Sometimes larger cats such as tigers or lions may kill a leopard. These big cats do not usually hunt leopards to eat. Instead, they may kill leopards to keep them from hunting prey that they will go after for themselves.

Although they don't have to worry about other predators, leopards do face dangers. The numbers of wild clouded leopards and snow leopards are falling quickly. As a result, these cats are now considered endangered species. Although many common leopards still remain in Africa, their numbers in Asia have gone down steadily in recent years.

Habitat Loss

The problems leopards face are a result of the increasing number of people who live in or near the

As human communities spread into once-wild areas, leopards are trapped to protect people from attacks.

leopards' habitat. As more and more people settle wild places, they change the environment for the leopards living there. Clouded leopards that live in tropical forests are facing the greatest changes in their habitat. The trees of tropical forests are being cut down to provide people with firewood and lumber. Clearing the forest land also creates places for people to build farms, roads, and houses. But without the trees in the forest, leopards have fewer places to hunt and rest. The animals that leopards hunt also become more rare when the forest is destroyed.

A leopard watches a herd of cattle in Kenya. Farmers often try to kill leopards to protect their livestock.

Many countries have set aside wild land as protected places where leopards and other wildlife can live. In some areas, these national parks and wildlife reserves are often the only safe pockets of habitat remaining for leopards. But as their habitat shrinks, leopards are squeezed into protected areas too small to provide all of the cats living there with the food and shelter they need. When that happens, some leopards die and the total number of leopards falls.

People and Livestock

Even leopards that live in protected wild habitats such as national parks have problems. Leopards often cross over the borders of parks and find themselves in conflict with people outside. The most serious problems occur when leopards attack people. Although snow leopards and clouded leopards have not been known to attack people, attacks by common leopards do take place.

Much more common than leopard attacks on people are attacks on livestock. Often leopards living outside of protected areas turn to killing cattle, goats, and sheep when they can no longer find their natural prey. Sometimes leopards that are old or injured will target livestock because it is easier for them to kill than wild animals.

Snow leopards are well known for killing sheep and goats tended by people living in villages high in Asia's mountains. For the snow leopard, the sight of rock corrals holding flocks of goats is a strong temptation. In a single night, one snow leopard can easily kill an entire herd. To protect their animals, villagers will kill snow leopards whenever possible.

Scientists have begun working with villagers in Asia to help them protect their livestock so they will not have a reason to kill snow leopards. They are teaching people how to build stronger, more protected goat corrals that snow leopards cannot enter. They have also provided guard dogs to protect the herds from attack. Through these actions, scientists hope that both people and snow leopards will be able to live safely in the same areas.

Poaching

While some people kill leopards out of fear for their own safety or that of their livestock, others kill leopards for money. Although most countries have laws that protect leopards from hunters, illegal hunting is common in many places. This illegal hunting is known as **poaching** and is a serious threat to all three types of leopards.

Leopards are often poached for their beautiful spotted fur. These furs are sold in markets, usually to be made into fur coats for people to wear. Even though it is against the law to sell furs made from endangered species, coats made from clouded leopard and snow leopard skins can often be found in Asian markets. Because these furs can sell for large amounts of money, poachers are willing to take the risk of getting arrested. Recently, however, the wearing of leopard coats has become less popular as more people realize that the cats are becoming rare.

As people have stopped wearing fur coats, poachers have turned to selling other parts of the bodies of leopards that they kill. Recently, leopard teeth, claws, and bones have become even more valuable than leopard furs. These body parts are usually ground up for use in medicines. Adding ingredients from wild animals to medicine is an old tradition in Asia. Many people believe that by drinking a potion made from the

Although in many places it is illegal to hunt leopards, poachers like these hunt the cats for their valuable fur.

Rare and valuable leopard pelts are still sold illegally in some parts of Asia and Africa.

bones of a leopard they will become strong and brave like the cat. These beliefs, developed over many thousands of years, are very difficult to change. Scientists worry that poaching for traditional medicines might cause leopards to disappear from Asia in the near future.

Studying Leopards

Many scientists are working to find ways to protect leopards before it is too late. In order to protect leopards, scientists must first learn as much as possible about their habits. However, leopards are very difficult to study. Because they are very alert and shy, they usually stay far away from people. Therefore, scientists usually are not able to watch leopards in person. Instead, they will use special tools that allow them to watch leopards from a distance.

One such tool is the camera trap. Instead of actually capturing leopards, camera traps "capture" photographs of leopards. To take these photographs, scientists set up cameras along animal trails in the forest or mountainside. Each camera sends an invisible beam of light across the trail. When an animal walks through the beam of light, the camera takes a photograph.

These photographs show scientists the many different animals that pass along the trail, including leopards and their prey. Because no two leopards have the same pattern of spots on their coats, scientists can recognize individual animals from the photographs and count how many leopards they saw. Based on that number, the scientists can determine how many leopards live in the area.

Tracking Leopards

Another way scientists watch cats from a distance is by radio tracking. To radio track a leopard a scientist captures the cat and attaches a special collar around its neck. This collar will give out a signal that the scientist can listen to using special equipment. Once the leopard is released back into the forest the scientist will be able to track its movements.

Scientists fit a radio collar on the neck of a tranquilized leopard.

Once the leopard wakes up, the collar will allow experts to track the animal's movements.

With information from both camera traps and radio tracking scientists can learn how much space and what kind of habitat each leopard needs to be safe. This knowledge helps with decisions on what areas should be set aside for protecting leopards.

The Future of Leopards

By learning more about leopards, scientists hope to reduce some of the problems that threaten their future. Leopards are designed by nature to hunt and kill other animals. However, this design makes it difficult for leopards to fit into the modern world with growing numbers of people. But people have the power to take action to make sure that leopards will always have a future.

GLOSSARY

ambush: To attack suddenly, without warning.

caching: Storing food for later use.

camouflage: The ability to blend into the surrounding environment to hide from predators or prey.

canine teeth: Long, fanglike teeth in a cat's mouth.

carnassial teeth: Sharp cutting teeth on the sides of a cat's jaw.

carnivore: An animal that eats meat.

endangered species: An animal that is so rare that it might disappear in the near future.

gorge: To eat a great deal in a single meal.

habitat: The environment in which an animal lives.

incisors: The teeth at the front of the jaws.

nocturnal: Active at night.

panther: A black leopard.

poaching: Illegal hunting.

prey: An animal hunted and eaten by another animal.

retractable claws: Claws that can be withdrawn into a cat's paws.

rosette: A group of spots forming a circle.

species: A scientific classification used to label and identify groups of related plants or animals.

stalk: To sneak up slowly without being detected.

FOR FURTHER EXPLORATION

Books

Sandra Markle, *Outside and Inside Big Cats*. New York: Atheneum, 2002. A book full of photographs and information on wild cats, with a strong focus on how they hunt and kill their prey.

Jonathan and Angela Scott, *Big Cat Diary: Leopard*. London: HarperCollins UK, 2004. A companion to the *Big Cat Diary* television series, this book follows the lives of individual leopards living in the game parks of Africa. The authors provide a look into the leopards' daily activities and conservation needs.

Seymour Simon, *Big Cats*. New York: Harper Trophy, 1994. This book is an introduction to the big cats. Through photographs and text, it describes where they live, how they hunt, and how they care for their young.

Bernard Stonehouse, *A Visual Introduction to Wild Cats*. New York: Checkmark Books, 1999. One of the Animal Watch series, this book contains colorful pictures and information on each of the three leopard species.

Sarah Walker, *Big Cats*. New York: DK, 2002. This easy-to-read book is a basic introduction to the world of wild cats.

Websites

The Clouded Leopard Project (www.cloudedleop ard.org). Visit this website to learn more about how clouded leopards hunt, their lives in the forest, and their conservation needs.

The Snow Leopard Conservancy (www.snow leopardconservancy.org). Visit this website to learn about snow leopards and discover what people are doing to protect this endangered cat.

Cats: Plan for Perfection (www.nationalgeo graphic.com/cats). This interactive National Geographic site contains information on cat biology and behavior.

INDEX

PICTURE CREDITS

ABOUT THE AUTHOR

Karen D. Povey has spent her career as a conservation educator, working to instill an appreciation for wildlife in people of all ages. Karen makes her home in Tacoma, Washington, where she manages and presents live animal education programs at Point Defiance Zoo & Aquarium. Karen also participates in wild cat conservation efforts through her work with the Clouded Leopard Species Survival Plan® and the Clouded Leopard Project.